Henry Thompson Stanton

The Moneyless Man

And other Poems

Henry Thompson Stanton

The Moneyless Man
And other Poems

ISBN/EAN: 9783744739900

Printed in Europe, USA, Canada, Australia, Japan

Cover: Foto ©Andreas Hilbeck / pixelio.de

More available books at **www.hansebooks.com**

THE MONEYLESS MAN

AND OTHER POEMS

BY

HENRY T STANTON

BALTIMORE

HENRY C TURNBULL Jr

1871

This Volume

IS

DEDICATED

TO

MY MOTHER.

CONTENTS.

THE MONEYLESS MAN.

Is there no secret place on the face of the earth,
Where charity dwelleth, where virtue has birth?
Where bosoms in mercy and kindness will heave,
When the poor and the wretched shall ask and
    receive?
Is there no place at all, where a knock from the
    poor,
Will bring a kind angel to open the door?
Ah, search the wide world wherever you can
There is no open door for a Moneyless Man!

Go, look in yon hall where the chandelier's light
Drives off with its splendor the darkness of night,
Where the rich-hanging velvet in shadowy fold
Sweeps gracefully down with its trimmings of gold,
And the mirrors of silver take up, and renew,
In long lighted vistas the 'wildering view :
Go there ! at the banquet, and find, if you can,
A welcoming smile for a Moneyless Man !

Go, look in yon church of the cloud-reaching spire,
Which gives to the sun his same look of red fire,
Where the arches and columns are gorgeous within,
And the walls seem as pure as a soul without sin ;
Walk down the long aisles, see the rich and the great
In the pomp and the pride of their worldly estate ;
Walk down in your patches, and find, if you can,
Who opens a pew to a Moneyless Man.

Go, look in the Banks, where Mammon has told
His hundreds and thousands of silver and gold ;
Where, safe from the hands of the starving and poor,
Lies pile upon pile of the glittering ore !
Walk up to their counters — ah, there you may stay
'Til your limbs grow old, 'til your hairs grow gray,
And you 'll find at the Banks not one of the clan
With money to lend to a Moneyless Man !

Go, look to yon Judge, in his dark-flowing gown,
With the scales wherein law weigheth equity down ;
Where he frowns on the weak and smiles on the
        strong,
And punishes right whilst he justifies wrong ;
Where juries their lips to the Bible have laid,
To render a verdict — they 've already made :
Go there, in the court-room, and find, if you can,
Any law for the cause of a Moneyless Man !

Then go to your hovel — no raven has fed
The wife who has suffered too long for her bread ;

Kneel down by her pallet, and kiss the death-frost
From the lips of the angel your poverty lost:
Then turn in your agony upward to God,
And bless, while it smites you, the chastening rod,
And you 'll find, at the end of your life's little span,
There 's a welcome above for a Moneyless Man!

NAMELESS.

THERE were great lights from the palace
  Streaming on the outer trees,
That, with fleckings thro' the trellis,
  Played a-tremor at his knees,
As a minstrel stranger, friendless,
  Underneath the walls of Fame
Sat in silence, whilst the endless
  Notes of glory-music came.

Paths, to him, were bleak and aimless,
  As he sat within the shade,
Telling o'er the wonders, nameless,
  That his poet-heart had made :
" Could he pass the amber portal,
  And the jasper halls along,
Where the poet-souls immortal
  Held their revelry of song?

" Could he strike a chord of sorrow
  In the upper, choral spheres,
Where to-morrow, and to-morrow,
  It would echo down the years?

Could he grasp the ivy clinging
    At the marble casement, now,
And amid the spirits singing,
    Wear it, deathless, on his brow?"

Once he thought to climb the terrace
    To the open, opal gate,
Where, beyond the sweeping arras,
    Swelled the voices of the great;
Where the stricken harp-strings golden
    Gave their notes in high accord
To the music-stories olden,
    To the glory of the LORD.

But his soul, untaught and simple,
    Shrinking outward, turned away,
Where the great lights from the temple
    Drove the night-time from the day:
"I shall seek the shadow, yonder
    Underneath the silent pine;
There are harp-notes higher, grander
    Than may ever be from mine!"

Soft he touched the strings, like Summer
    Touching o'er the barren trees,
And the night bore out their murmur,
    Through its alleys, to the seas;
Softer, sweeter went the cadence
    Through the branches and above,

B

As come visions unto maidens
   In the budding-time of love.

Through the gates of opal splendor,
   And along the jasper wall,
Pass the notes of music tender,
   Through the corridor and hall;
And his tones sweep in the chamber
   From the shadow and the gloom,
And their liquid echoes clamber
   Up the arras to the dome.

And they rise and fall like billows,
   In the alcoves of the air,
Passing in and out the willows,
   And across beyond the mere;
High, and grand, and godly power
   Sweeps along the palace eaves,
'Til the ivy-vine, in flower,
   Trembles music from its leaves.

And the poet-souls may listen
   To the outer harp to-night,
And the great lamps gleam and glisten
   In an ecstacy of light;
These are music-tones undying,
   These are worthy highest name,
From the poet-spirit lying
   Underneath the walls of Fame.

CASTE.

If, as a burn,
That from the shadow fleeing,
Seeks the shine
On some broad river,
I now could turn
The current of my being
Into thine,
To flow forever —
Believest thou this tribute-blood
Would give thy veins to darker flood?

The tuneful brooks
That down the slopes are going
To the sea
With music-laughter,
In hidden nooks
Begin their silver flowing,
Silently,
To chorus after.
Believest thou, because obscure
Of origin, they are not pure?

Not in the grand,
Resistless, moving river,
Do we find
The lucent crystal ;
But out the land
The springs run limpid ever,
Overtwined
By vine and thistle :
Not from the pure, pearled fountain veins
Do rivers take their *débris* stains.

O, maid !   O, queen !
O, proud and pulsing woman !
If the tide
That floods these valleys,
Less pure were seen
Than that in any human,
It should hide
In covert alleys,
Where cunning eyes should never trace
The slow course of its under-race.

THE NASTURTIUM FLOWER.

I saw, last night, a ruin gray,
    An isolated tower,
A work of art, from which decay
Had crumbled portions every day,
    A feature, every hour ;

And o'er it grew a summer vine,
    A purple Morning Glory,
That hung in many a waving line,
And many a clustering tassel fine,
    From turrets old and hoary ;

And underneath the ruined wall,
    In moody spirit lying,
I saw the white wave rise and fall,
And heard the sea-bird's mystic call,
    Far on the waters dying.

The wood upon the sombre hill
    Its leafy bosom hushes,
And nothing wakes the midnight still,
Save here and there a Whip-po-wil
    From widely scattered bushes.

I know not if my eyelids fell —
 My pulses were not failing ;
I saw the ocean's even swell ;
At intervals, my ear could tell
 The lone bird's far-off wailing.

And while I lay, with wandering eye
 O'er Heaven's starry arches,
And watched the meteor shooting by,
And saw the Pleiads holding high
 Their ever-burning torches,

A voice came from the ruin old,
 At first, a pleasant murmur ;
And then I heard a story told
In accents stronger, and more bold,
 Of Winter and of Summer.

The Vine said to the Tower gray:
 " My leaves about thee flinging,
Thou shalt not feel the burning day,
Thy rocks shall never waste away
 Where my green arms are clinging.

" Uphold me with thy sturdy hand,
 And lift me from the shadow,
And thou shalt feel thy gray brow fanned
With zephyrs, through its leafy band,
 From fragrant field and meadow.

" I 'll gather all the morning dew
  Within my purple flower,'
And when the sun comes up anew,
I 'll wash thy granite bosom true
  With all my silvery shower.

" So tenderly I 'll twine around
  Each fragment, trembling over,
That it shall spurn the colder ground,
And feel itself as sweetly bound
  As lady to her lover.

" I 'll make thy portal emerald-green,
  With here and there a blossom,
And thou shalt have some fairy queen
To come into my leaves, and lean
  Her forehead on thy bosom.

" Oh, I will make thy life so sweet,
  In one delightful Summer,
That pulses in thy heart shall beat
And then — I 'll wither at thy feet,
  And die without a murmur."

Then spoke the cold gray stones, and said :
  " Thy life, sweet Vine, is golden ;
The season all its charms has shed
Upon thy fair and fragile head,
  While I am gray and olden.

"I need not tell thee whence I sprung;
  For yonder craggy mountain
Is not more old, nor yet more young,
Although its brows have frowning hung
  Since Adam, o'er the fountain.

"My form is rude, as thine is fair;
  My limbs are cold and cheerless;
I feel the very summer air
Come searching through me, even where
  Thou cling'st in beauty peerless.

"No zephyr comes but takes away
  A portion of my being;
The gathered dew, that starry spray
Which thou upon my breast would'st lay,
  But aids my life in fleeing.

"The sunshine through thy very leaves
  My particles doth sever;
And while thy tender bosom grieves,
One after one an atom leaves,
  And I am dying ever.

"The summer rain that bids thee live,
  And opens out thy blossom,
Can to my life no freshness give,
But takes away the strength I have
  In passage through my bosom.

"Oh, I have seen a form like thine
 Reach up — how very often ! —
And here its gentle tendrils twine
About this frosty head of mine,
 As thou, my cares to soften.

"And I have seen the Autumn too
 The fairest trellis redden ;
And Winter, pour its breathing through
The very cup that caught the dew.
 And all its powers deaden.

"And one by one their lives have fled,
 As thine will soon be flying ;
And at my feet a fragrant bed
Of withered leaves, and tendrils dead,
 In sorrow will be lying.

"I cannot weep, though all I love,
 The freshest and the fairest,
That on my gray rocks live and move,
Must take the garb that Winter wove
 For that which now thou wearest.

"The Winters come, and come and go,
 And I am here repining ;
I feel alike the sun and snow,
The zephyr or the storms that blow,
 Where thy green arms are twining."

The voices hushed, and silence came,
A spell upon the Heaven;
And underneath the Pleiad's flame,
The mantled tower stood the same;
The ocean swelled as even.

I prithee, lady, read my dream
To thine interpretation,
And it shall take that brighter gleam
From thy poetic current stream,
To music's sweet relation.

In blessing me it must have been,
At that enchanted hour,
That thou, of fay and blossom kin,
Had left a spirit sleeping in
The bosom of the flower.

And thus to me in vision thrall
Came glories without number:
I see the white wave rise and fall,
I hear the sea-bird's mystic call
In echoes from my slumber.

Ah, unto such a soul as mine
The gentle fairy's doin'
Was but to tell in softer line,
That thou wert yet a tender vine,
And I a crumbled ruin!

WINTER NIGHT.

WHEN the soul is weary, weary,
Through these winter days so dreary,
　　With their wilderness of white,
There's a charm for such an illness
In the shadow and the stillness
　　Of the sober, thoughtful night.

When the earth's green shoots are dying,
And the cold snow o'er them flying —
　　Flying all the Winter day,
Then the heart will beat in sadness,
While with strange, fantastic gladness
　　The white flakes seem to play.

But the purple Night comes, slowly,
As some abbess, grave and holy,
　　Up the still aisles of the sky;
And the red stars troop the arches
With their legions, to the marches
　　That are only heard on high.

Then the soul, no longer minion,
Beats the trammels from its pinion,
    Bids its sorrow all adieu ;
And the scarcely dying even,
Sees in yonder tranquil Heaven
    Its white wing cleaving through.

THE LIFE-WAY.

THE axe-man of life, at the Master's decree,
Hath come from the clearing and girdled a tree —
An oak that was leaning in sympathy o'er
The ashes of trees that were girdled before ;
And under our feet, as the passage we tread,
The branches are withered, the blossoms are dead.

Before is a forest, behind is a plain
Where verdure may never be trodden again ;
For, on to the shadow and into the shade,
We follow the way that the woodman has made :
Though sturdy the monarchs, and stately and tall,
The axe of the woodman must girdle them all.

The forest is Life, and the trees are the Years,
The leaves under-foot are the symbols of tears,
And shadows are with us wherever we go,
And spirits are weary and eyelids a-flow ;
For TIME is the woodman, and over his track
The feet of humanity never go back.

  * * * * * *

There are those in the world, who, living too fast,
Have never an eye for the lesson-full past,
But in reaching beyond and peering away,
They trample the bloom that environs to-day,
And suffer with hope, and out of their sorrow
They rush to the ultimate pang of to-morrow.

The pleasures we seek and the jewels we find
Are never before, but are ever behind ;
And carelessly, heedlessly still do we pass
The treasure-full things that go down in the glass ;
For the greed of a greater thing urgeth us on
'Til gem after gem in the life-sand is gone.

Our moments are gold, and the shores of the Past
From whence we have come on the journey too fast,
Are sparkled with riches we never may reach,
That lay in our way as we loitered the beach —
When Hope went ahead with its promises sweet,
We trampled Reality under our feet.

As bees go over
The seas of clover,
So do my heart-wings go to my lover;
  And over the grades
  Of murmurous blades,
And over the shimmer and over the shades,
  And airy and light
  As a fairy's flight,
I follow the arc of the inner sight.

  Where a commerce moves
  In its iron grooves,
May tarry the clay of the heart that loves;
  But over the aisles
  Of the iron miles
Must hasten the eye to the eye that smiles;
  To the jewel set
  In a minaret
The track of its gleam is the truest yet.

27

I.

In Mason's Hall, with earnest eyes,
  Upon the Chart before me,
I viewed the symboled mysteries
That Masons keep and Masons prize;
I see the arm my brothers wield,
Uplifted with its burnished shield,
  Let fall its shadow o'er me.

II.

My sisters true — in years agone —
  Beyond the waste of water
I see them stand and beck me on:
Sweet RUTH, the gleaner at the dawn;
ELECTA, dear, and MARTHA wait;
Queen ESTHER, in her robes of State;
  And JEPHTHA'S peerless DAUGHTER!

28

III.

JUDGES, xi : 35.

" My father's vow, so fervent made,
  I would not have it broken!
And though my pallid neck be laid
All bare beneath the colder blade,
I 'll give him still a steadfast eye
And joy, in hearing as I die,
  ' Alas ! my daughter ! ' spoken.
In Heaven's sight my faith I plight,
And I will break it never :
I 'll trust in *this*, and *this*, and *this*,
  Forever and forever ! "

IV.

RUTH ii : 5.

" The Master in the harvest days
  Shall find me gleaning early ;
The sun shall gild me with his rays
As I go down the reaper ways,
And tho' He ask, ' Whose damsel 's this ? '
I know His great heart cannot miss
  These little hands of barley.
In Heaven's sight my faith I plight,
  And I will break it never :
I 'll trust in *this*, and *this*, and *this*,
  Forever and forever ! "

V.

ESTHER, V : 3.

" I fearless go before the crown
　　To move the thorns that fester ;
And though the king himself may frown,
And long to cut God's people down,
I still have faith in such a day
That he will smile and freely say,
　' What wilt thou, proud Queen Esther ? '
In Heaven's sight my faith. I plight,
　　And I will break it never :
I 'll trust in *this*, and *this*, and *this*,
　　Forever and forever ! "

VI.

JOHN, xi : 26.

" My faith in Christ no earthly hand
　　Can ever move or sever :
Go, take His tidings thro' the land
With cymbals loud and trumpets grand !
For He shall say, ' Believest this ? '
And dead shall rise His feet to kiss
　　Forever and forever !
In Heaven's sight my faith I plight,
　　And I will break it never :
I 'il trust in *this*, and *this*, and *this*,
　　Forever and forever ! "

VII.

2D Epis. John, ii : 5.

"Tho' rack and torture come to me —
    To husband, children, mother —
Thro' Jesus' blood I yet shall see
Some glimpses of eternity ;
And far beyond the cross — the grave —
There 's still a hand to bless and save
    For *loving one another.*
In Heaven's sight my faith I plight,
    And I will break it never :
I 'll trust in *this*, and *this*, and *this*,
    Forever and forever ! "

VIII.

" In virtue's paths my way shall be,
    Where flowers bloom the rarest ;
And all I know, and all I see,
Shall mark a sister's truth in me.
By yon bright star that shines above,
My path I 'll keep, and try to prove,
    Among ten thousand fairest.
In Heaven's sight my faith I plight,
    And I will break it never :
I 'll hope in *these*, and *these*, and *these*,
    Forever and forever ! "

Looking backward for the glory
  Of a gilded summer dawn,
Down a weary waste of whiteness —
  Down a dreary winter lawn ;
Looking backward for the freshness
  Of a green and sapful June,
Through the sombre brown and crimson
  Of an autumn afternoon ;
Looking backward, down the shadow
  Of an iron-beaten way,
Whence the armored Time came, silent,
  On this animate to day.
O, it startles human reason,
  O, it withers human pride —
Looking backward, ever backward,
  For the living things that died ;
And the soul that seems immortal
  In the never-breaking gloom,
Hath a presence at the portal
  Of the palace of the tomb.

DEAD FLOWERS.

" Because I wore them for an hour,
    Forever fresh to thee."

THE Rose-bud on thy bosom died —
    O, death, divinely sweet —
Whilst here a poet-heart hath sighed,
To bear to thee its passion tide,
    And perish at thy feet.

The Fuchsia withered on thy brow,
    Amidst thy shining hair;
Whilst here a soul to earth would bow,
And break its latest altar-vow
    For but one moment there.

O, brow of pearl! O, breast of snow!
    O, lips of love divine!
The bud hath caught their crimson glow,
And borne thy pulse's tidal flow
    In purple life to mine.

33

BRING me a coal for my old clay pipe —
  A coal that is glowing and red,
    And draw up my chair
    To the fireside there,
  And hasten the children to bed :
We have finished our task and finished our tea,
  And the evening prayer is said.

Now place at the hearth a faggot or two,
  And carry the kettle away ;
    I'm thinking, my wife,
    Of the pleasure in life
  We have known this many a day ;
For our hearts are warm and our spirits young,
  Though our heads be turning gray.

Ah, now you look, with your knitting, there,
  So cheerful and pleasant, my dear,
    That I feel, full well,
    My old heart swell
  As it did in its bridal gear,
And I know it throbs as faithful still
  In the Autumn-time that's here.

Come back with me to the early day,
   The Spring of our tender love,
     When a fair young bride,
     At the altar-side,
   Looked up to the Heaven above,
And God was nigh, and His Summer wind
   Sang joyous in the grove.

Our fathers were there, our mothers too —
   We cherish the blessings they gave ;
     And tears must fall
     To know they 're all
   In the cold and silent grave,
     Where the slow years pass
     In the dropping glass,
And willows o'er them wave.

But all of us die, and day by day
   We pillow each other to sleep,
     And the tears may rise
     To our saddened eyes
   From the heart in its sorrow deep ;
But God hath an eye to the sparrow's fall,
   And the humblest soul will keep.

For two score years we have kept our faith,
   And true to our earliest tryst,
     We have found the goal
     Of a quiet soul,

That many a heart hath missed,
And many a spirit hath wandered away
   To the tones we would not list.

Ah, wife, I feel my old blood course
   And tingle away in my veins,
     When I think how true
     Both I and you,
   Together, have guided the reins,
With nothing on earth to mar our love,
   And fret and bother our brains.

And here we sit, on this Winter night,
   A cozy and happy old pair,
     And loving as true
     As we used to do
   When I was young and you were fair,
And the silver thread from the loom of years
   Came not in your raven hair.

I shake the coal from my old clay pipe,
   For now it is blackened and dead,
     And the faggot gone,
     And the fire wan,
   And the lamp-wick nearly fled,
And the clock, with a nervous stroke, says TEN
   And it's time to go to bed!

UNDER THE PINES.

Night, with her clustering, coronal stars,
Over a world full of passions and wars
　　Her quieting wing has spread ;
There 's silence out in these mystical hills —
There 's silence over the voiceful rills,
And Earth, to all of its sorrowful thrills
　　In the fever of day, is dead.

O, beautiful Night! sweet season of dreams!
Rich in thy glory and soft in thy gleams,
　　How rapidly fleeting thou art!
Throw over my spirit thy mantle of gold,
Let slumber and visions my bosom enfold,
Till all of thine eloquent moments are told
　　In the silvery sands of my heart.

Out in the meadow are those who have died,
The stream running still from the wound open wide —
　　Oh, I sickened all day at the sight!
Alas! for the heart of its idol denied!
Alas! for the vow of the groom to the bride!
He only may come to her tremulous side
　　In the beautiful visions of Night!

D

SHE.

O, COLD are the flakes
That fall in the lakes,
And bitter the winds that be ;
And icy and chill
The minarets still
That stand in the Polar Sea;

But colder than all
Of the flakes that fall,
And the bitterest winds that be —
Than the *Mer de glace*
In the Northern Pass —
Than the Pole itself — is she.

In the amber light
Of the sky, one night,
I tore my bosom apart,
And under a moon
Of the fervid June
Was "offered" to her my heart;

For I tore it out
Of its red redoubt,

And laid it over the pyre,
    Where the torrid heat
    Of its fever-beat
Went, soul to soul, with the fire.

    But never a stone
    To the chisel known
So little of pulse betrayed,
    And the passion-lines
    Of her outer signs
Meant — never a word they said.

    O, the glacier stoop
    Of her shoulders' droop
May show in the night like gold,
    And the lunar fleck
    On her marble neck
A tinge of the blood may hold;

    But never a drop
    Of the venous cup
Can ever the lancet shed :
    The fever has flown —
    The woman is stone,
And the sylph-like thing is dead.

    What the boddice robes
    For her mammal globes
Is only an icy lie;

Though the lace may rest
On her milk-white breast,
A babe at the place would die!

For colder than all
Of the flakes that fall,
And the bitterest winds that be —
Than the *Mer de glace*
In the Northern Pass —
Than the Pole itself — is she!

HER whiter hand lay lost in mine,
The while she turned away
To where the evening's flush of wine
Went up the face of day —
"When all these Autumn leaves are shed,
And I beyond the sea,
You 'll not forget, O Love," I said,
"The faith you 've plighted me?"

Her brown eyes, going outward far,
Were silent in reply;
It seemed she thought some early star
Would break the shadowed sky;
"When seeds of Spring are harvest grain,
And leaves in purple be,
You 'll not forget," I said again,
"The faith you 've plighted me?"

And shadows thickened where we stood,
And night came on apace;

I saw a tear — the heart's true blood —
   Stand silent on her face
" By these two hands at parting met,
   By sacred tears I see,
I know, dear Love, you 'll not forget
   The faith you 've plighted me."

Then came her full-heart from her eyes,
   Turned, liquidly, to mine —
" Did Eve forget her Paradise
   Beneath another vine?
No, no," she said, " the waves may fling
   Their whiteness on the sea,
Nor time, nor tide, nor death shall bring
   Forgetfulness to me!"

   *   *   *   *   *   *

I went where science, learning, art,
   Heaped memorable piles :
I felt the great world's pulsing heart
   Throb in the Flower Isles ;
I saw the countless soulful eyes
   That sparkle in their dance,
Beneath the rich Italian skies,
   The fruity hills of France ;

The Scottish truth — the Irish grace —
   The German's frugal care —

In every shape the human face,
　And beauty everywhere;
And Summer and the Autumn came,
　And leaves were in their fall—
I held her image here the same,
　An idol over all.

*　　　*　　　*　　　*　　　*　　　*

You mark the pale, proud woman there.
　Beneath the astral shine:
Despite such blossoms in her hair
　Her heart should pulse to mine:
I brought the sunset back to-night
　From far beyond the sea;
I dared not think she held so light
　The faith she plighted me!

I clutched the goblet as a vise,
　And pledged her thus in wine:
May Eve forget her Paradise
　Beneath another vine!
And then I said, the waves may fling
　Their whiteness on the sea,
Nor time, nor tide, nor death shall bring
　Forgetfulness to me!

O, friend! I trust no siren tongue,
　No human voice or tears;

In all the world I dwelt among,
  No eye had truth like hers.
I pass no more the blighted spot,
  No more the shadows see,
Since she who loved so soon forgot
  The faith she plighted me!

CHARITY.

How many proud people who gather to-day
In chambers of pleasure, at feasts of display,
Who quicken their lips in immaculate wine,
With its typical foam and its sparkle divine,
Have a pang at the heart, or a tear at the eye,
For the woman in rags who is shivering by?

How many to-day in this legion of souls
Who are tracing the pictures that glow in the coals,
Who see in the future their temples arise
As the wonderful homes unto worshipful eyes,
Have pulses awake for the shadowy poor,
Who, white as the marble, enphantom the door?

How many, O God! in Thy mercy and grace,
Who are made in Thy form and are stamped with
    Thy face,

45

Who move on Thy footstool, and graciously live
With light for Thy worship, with power to give,
Have oil for the wounds of the man by the way,
Or bread to be cast on the waters to-day?

O, people whose chambers of crimson and gold
Are astir with the lambs of your own little fold,
Whose feet in their frolic just dimple the bed
Of the burying velvet the little ones tread,
Be still for a season, just hearken the moans
Of the poor little feet that are bare on the stones!

O, people who banquet, and revel, and laugh
In the blood of the grape and the fat of the calf;
When dwelling in plenty and swelling in pride
Your children are petted, and pampered, and plied,
Throw open your casements, and look at the brood,
Just over the way, who are crying for food!

O, people in coaches, with liveried things
That wait in the glitter of tinsel and rings,
That come at your becking and go at your will —
All creatures of Mammon—God's images still!—
Sink back in your cushions and hide you in shame
From the piteous eyes of the paupered and lame!

O, mistress of fashion! O, master of gold!
Far hidden in furs from the sting of the cold —
As your spirits go out and your ecstasy swells

At the sight of the snow and the sound of the bells,
Do you mind that the widow is wanting a cloak —
That her chimney is bleak in a city of smoke?

Come out of your casings, O, armor-clad souls,
That live in the tinkle of ewers and bowls;
Come out from the sight of your carpeted feet
With pity for those that are bare in the street:
Come, open your coffers, in mercy, to-day,
For the little ones crying just over the way!

Step out of your coaches and cutters, O, fools
That sneer at the wretches that dwell in the pools;
Step out, and for once in the bountiful year
Have eyes that can see and have ears that can
  hear;
Step out from your cushions of revel and shame —
Go comfort the widow, go pity the lame!

O, there's nothing at all in this region below
So hollow and dead as their tinsel and show;
When people who shimmer in glory and gold
Are blind to the beings that dwell in the cold;
When lights from their windows, that dazzle the
  poor,
See most of true virtue outside of the door!

O, blessings for people, who, feasting to-day,
Have thought of the little ones over the way;

Whose spirits, grown large at the board and the
      hearth,
Cry welcome, to all the distressed of the earth!
O, blessings for people, who, hearing their moans,
Have lifted the bare-footed out of the stones!

SEVENTY.

The sad Sixty-nine in the midnight has gone,
And Seventy comes in his chariot on ;
With light in his eye and a flush in his face,
He enters the course and is in for the race.
A fever of being, a fullness of joy
Is throbbing the pulse of the animate boy.
'Tis a glorious hope that his spirit reveals
In the crack of his whip and the rush of his wheels.

* * * * * *

But life is a mockery — common decay
Is big in the womb of the promising day ;
For death hath a touch at the heart of the corn
Ere light on the silk of its tassel is born ;
And never a flower abandons the dust
But foldeth a germ of the cankering rust ;
And even the beautiful, bountiful year
That cometh to-day in its infancy here,
Is typed in the life of ephemeral bloom,
For he driveth his chariot on to the tomb.

F

In the glow of a purple October —
  The nut-dropping time of the year —
When leaves have a rustle of splendor,
  And branches in silver appear,
As cometh the sun to the Sabbath,
  Up out of the Orient hills,
A sense of an Infinite Being
  The whole of humanity fills.

Man sees in the passage of seasons,
  The regular transit of days,
How great is Thy goodness, Jehovah !
  How wondrous, O God, are Thy ways !
The steeple-bells over the churches
  That dot, in their whiteness, the land,
Elate at the glad Sabbath morning,
  Ring out in a symphony grand ;
And homes that are sprinkled with children
  A story of happiness tells,

When faces grow bright at the music
  That flows from the Sabbath School bells.

Now out of the lane and the by-way,
  And out of the alley and street,
With murmurous mingle of voices
  And musical patter of feet,
The children of *all* of the people —
  The humble in state and the high,
The rich in their Astrachan wrappings,
  The poor in their woolen — go by.

And in at the arch of the chapel,
  Along in the sanctified aisles,
They gather like earliest blossoms
  That Spring in her beauty beguiles ;
And there, at the foot of the altar —
  A ground that is *even* at last —
The hearts of the children are measured
  By Heaven's true standard of caste.

The bells of the Sabbath are ringing
  Alike for the rich and the poor,
And open the mine of the Bible
  To all who are seeking its store :
No prince at the zenith of power,
  With nations on suppliant knees,
Hath gems in his coronal decking
  That sparkle in fervor like these.

Come hither, O children, and gather
  The jewels God scatters to-day ;
Here's Honor, and Virtue, and Mercy,
  The riches that never decay ;
Here's knowledge that's free to the orphan,
  The child of the widow may learn —
The prince and the pauper together
  May in at the vestibule turn.

Come, children, glad-eyed and white-hearte
  And join in an anthem of praise ;
Thank God for the voice in the steeple
  That heralds His holiest days ;
Thank God for the boon of the Bible,
  The blessed Redeemer of men,
The glorious plan of salvation
  Revealed in the beautiful Ten.

Away with sectarian uses,
  The narrow confinements of creed ;
The little one's heart is a garden
  Where Jesus should scatter the seed.
Teach God as a merciful Father,
  The source and the fountain of love ;
Not feared for His might, and the power
  He wields in the kingdom above,
But honored and glorified ever
  For Charity, Mercy, and Love,
The jewels to seek in the Bible
  And wear to the kingdom above.

These grey-bearded men of the city,
  Worn out in the service of trade,
Their foot-way, borne down from the sunlight,
  Is bent to the valley of shade ;
And stories of struggle and sorrow
  The lines in their faces can tell,
Since light-hearted children together
  They answered the Sabbath School bell.

And often and often at midnight
  Their memory goes to the past,
To wander again in the flowers
  That GOD in their passage had cast ;
And up from the glory of childhood,
  In mystical melody swells
A sound that endureth forever —
  The song of the Sabbath Day bells.

E *

TYPE AND TIME.

THAT stern old man, the Harvester.
    Who garners in the years,
Whose passage up the fields of space
    A path of death appears ;
Whose way is in the early grain
    Ere yet its golden hue,
And bended head, and parting husk,
    Invite the sickle through ;

That cold old man, whose arteries,
    At Mercy's plaint, congea¹
And harden, that they may but show
    The blood's organic steel —
He feels no pity, knows no shame,
    Nor spares nor passes o'er
An atom in the widening plain
    That, trackless, lies before.

He turns not back, but onward still,
    With steady, tireless sweep,

His burnished scythe goes through the realm
　　Forevermore to reap ;
No RUTH of Moab in his wake
　　With tender hands may glean,
Nor stem nor stalk shall stand for her
　　Where iron Time has been.

But stolid eye and tuneless ear
　　Shall quicken at a sound
That floats above the reaper sphere,
　　And spurns the harvest-ground ;
For Time shall note, beyond the dust
　　Of men and nations wrecked,
The stately tread of Genius,
　　And the march of Intellect.

Whoso hath marked the lives of men,
　　Their better words and deeds,
May point some flower blossoming
　　Above the trammel weeds ;
Some growth hath struggled out the arms
　　That undertwine the way,
And lifts its scented splendor
　　In the ardent upper day.

Though blight and blast may fell the stalk
　　In seasons urging by,
The essence of the flower still
　　Is floating on the sky ;

And free, beyond the reach of death,
  Upon the arch sublime,
The souls of men of Intellect
  And Genius conquer Time.

Go back along the shadow-days,
  And down their cycles run,
And mark the lights from human lives
  Since human lives begun :
Though countless legions in the throng
  Were stars that early set,
The grand old planets of the past
  Are at the zenith yet.

From out the darkness of an age
  That gave their genius birth,
They rose above the atmosphere
  And battled down the earth ;
And in the space, from every clime,
  And every class, are some
Who prove how under-gravity
  Is grandly overcome.

So let us live, and act, and be,
  That after-time may tell
We were not in the reaper-way,
  Nor by the sickle fell ;
But upward, over all that die,
  By force of human will,

We cut a passage to the sky
And hold the æther still.

*　　　*　　　*　　　*　　　*　　　*

On those who gather here to-day,
　　Some lights, that ever show,
Have come to shed their glory-ray
　　From out the long-ago :
The first old masters of an Art,
　　Ere Genius yet was ripe,
Who threw the cruder stylus down
　　To greet the coming Type ;

Who from the cells of hooded monks,
　　And sacrist scribes, and clerks,
Were free to bear the outer world
　　The magic of their works ;
Who tore the vail of mystery
　　From small Khorassans then
That swayed the world with vellum scraps
　　Of wisdom from the pen.

The German KOSTER, first of all,
　　Whose carven letters came
And gave the acts of noble men
　　To glory and to fame ;
Whose spirit, from the narrow groove
　　That circumscribed his kind,
Was bold to break the barrier
　　And poach the fields of mind.

The common chain that ignorance
   And superstition bound,
His light ambition scorned to wear
   Upon the trodden ground ;
And men were taught forevermore
   That better path to climb,
When KOSTER sent the Bible up
   The avenues of Time.

Though long ago his parchment sheets,
   And vellum scrolls, and leaves
Were gathered by the Harvester
   And lie among the sheaves,
We lift the science of his thought
   From out the rubbish lost,
With honor to old GUTTENBERG
   And gratitude to FAUST.

Where'er the cunning Type is known —
   Where'er the magic page
Is stamped with living characters
   That photograph the age,
The massive forms of GUTTENBERG,
   Of FAUST, and SCHŒFFER too,
Shall stalk the aisles of learning
   And the paths of genius through.

These are the planet-stars that shine
   For those who follow still

The science-way that leaves the vale
　And takes the stubborn hill;
These are the patron-saints — the gods
　Of energy and worth,
That point us from Apprenticeship
　To Mastery on earth.

And down the sparkled arch that bends
　Above these darker years,
We hail the risen splendor
　Of our later pioneers;
The noble FRANKLIN of our own,
　Whose hand of usefulness
Was first to clutch the thunderbolt
　And draw the lever-press.

The simple beauty of his life —
　The smooth and even pace
With which he took the upper way
　And won the honor race,
Have left, through reaching history
　And ever-ringing fame,
The civil world electrified
　And nervous with his name.

We hold the greatness of his brain,
　His openness and truth,
The highest model for our men,
　The noblest for our youth;

The brawn-armed daily laborer —
  The ermined of the State
May find, in FRANKLIN's excellence,
  A life to emulate.

And after him, above the verge,
  Our firmament can show
The advent of another star —
  The scintillating HOE!
The hot sheets from his cylinders
  O'er all the land are spread,
To tell the world how Intellect
  And Genius are not dead.

White-winged and free, across the sea
  His seeds of labor fly,
And men must know, where'er they go,
  How Genius cannot die ;
For all the soil of fertile brains
  With labor-seeds are rife —
They germinate in fields of fame,
  And in the sands of life.

As long as Christian temples bear
  Their turrets to the sun —
As long as in our cycle lives
  The sands of Fame shall run,
So long shall human hearts be glad,
  And human voices bless

The master-hands that wrought the Type
And reared the magic Press.

*   *   *   . *   *

For us, who stand as Signal-men,
    Along the army track,
And onward wave the messages,
    From flags that lessen back,
How meet it is that arm, and eye,
    Should steady be, and true,
To guard the honor of the post,
    And speed the signal through.

We hold the symbol of a cause,
    A power in our hands,
To point the army-march, and shape
    The destiny of lands ;
To good, or ill, we guide the world,
    By virtue of our trust —
For good, we lift the signal high —
    For ill, it trails the dust.

When, here and there, a veteran
    And leader in the corps,
Is signalled from the angel flags
    That flit the silent shore,
He musters out of human strife,
    And treads the courts of fate —
Our HARNEY's through the vestibule,
    Our PRENTICE at the gate.

F

God keep us in the goodly track,
    That leaves the ill behind !
God turn us to the flower-way
    Of love for humankind !
God give us grace to wield the PEN,
    And so direct the PRESS,
That we may point our fellow-men,
    To ever-blessedness !

And TIME may keep his steady sweep
    Throughout the fields of earth,
And in the maze of autumn days
    May fell the latest birth ;
But human souls have higher goals,
    Where reapers never dare,
And men shall rise beyond the skies,
    To shine forever there.

MOUNT VERNON.

MOUNT VERNON! dear, neglected spot,
   I mourn for what thou art —
A shapeless ruin and a blot
   Upon a nation's heart.

Thy withered leaf, thy tangled vine,
   Thy dying trees and nude,
Are but, alas! the common sign
   Of human gratitude.

Thy flowers all, that pleasures dear
   To WASHINGTON once gave,
Forsaken and neglected here,
   Have died upon his grave!

Who would not weep for very shame,
   His crumbling tomb beside?

To *him* a nation owes its fame,
  Its freedom and its pride!

To *him* the proudest king on earth
  Was bent submissive down;
He taught the world that Freedom's birth
  Was higher than the crown.

His life was not that transient gleam
  That fades within the grave —
The bubble on the placid stream,
  That bursts upon the wave;

But, like some fixed, eternal star,
  With steady, constant light,
His soul streams through the future far,
  Still glorious and bright!

And what tho' Vernon's flowers now
  In silent dust are laid?
The living wealth upon his brow
  Can never, never fade!

When thrones have fallen, empires died,
  Like leaves beneath the sun,
Thy name shall still be spoke with pride,
  IMMORTAL WASHINGTON!

Go plant fresh flowers by his grave!
  Go bid Mount Vernon smile!
And give to him, who Freedom gave,
  An everlasting pile!

F *

TYPES OF LIFE.

I saw a star fall from its home
In Heaven's blue and boundless dome,
    To gleam no more;
I saw a wave with snowy crest
'Thrown from the Ocean's stormy breast,
    Upon the shore.

I saw a rose of perfect bloom
Bend, fading to its wintry tomb
    In silent grief;
I saw a living oak, but now,
Touched by the storm, with shattered bough
    And withered leaf.

The star had shone thro' countless years,
And shed its rays like virgin tears,
    So pure and bright,
That earth scarce knew the holy thrall,
And only sighed to see it fall
    And fade in night.

66

The wave had wandered to and fro,
With Ocean's ebb and Ocean's flow,
    From pole to pole,
Till here upon the nameless strand
It sank beneath the thirsty sand,
    Its final goal!

The rose sprang from a fallen seed,
And smiled above the graceless weed,
    To greet the sun;
But 'neath the Winter's chilling breath,
The lovely flow'rets' race to death
    Was quickly run.

The living oak, with noble shade,
Had stood the monarch of the glade,
    Thro' ages long;
But rifted by the lightning's glare,
His sturdy arms grew brown and bare,
    And were not strong.

And these are types of human lives;
Man lives a little while and thrives,
    But withers fast.
He sees a thousand lovely gleams,
But wastes his life away in dreams,
    And falls at last.

THE PATH.

Just by the road we are journeying fast,
    Down to the Lake of Tears,
A blind old man has tottered at last,
Out of the Present into the Past,
    Over the brink of years.

What were his virtues, what were his crimes,
    Nobody cares to-day;
Once he was ours — now he is Time's —
For lives are but as murmuring chimes,
    Coming and going away.

Up on the hill there 's a patter of feet —
    A voice in the flowers wild;
Carelessly down to the busy street,
Many to pass, and many to meet,
    Rambles a little child.

68

This is "the dead man's son and heir"
    Coming along the road;
He gathers the lightest treasures there,
The violet bloom and crocus fair,
    Bearing a childish load.

Soon he will be in the hurrying crowd,
    Pushing his way ahead —
Some of them broken — some of them bowed,
Some for the altar and some for the shroud,
    Some who are leading and led.

Soon in the way to the Lake of Tears,
    The little one's feet must go;
For thorns are thick in the path of years,
And the way to death is a way of fears,
    All down to the silent flow.

THE BIVOUAC.

A SOLDIER lay on the frozen ground,
With only a blanket tightened around
 His weary and wasted frame ;
Down at his feet, the fitful light
Of fading coals in the freezing night
Fell as a mockery on the sight,
 A heatless, purple flame.

All day long, with his heavy load,
Weary and sore, in the mountain road,
 And over the desolate plain ;
All day long, through the crusted mud,
Over the snow, and through the flood,
Marking his way with a track of blood
 He followed the winding train.

Nothing to eat at the bivouac
But a frozen crust in his haversack —

The half of a comrade's store —
A crust, that, after a longer fast,
Some pampered spaniel might have passed,
Knowing that morsel to be the last
    That lay at his master's door.

No other sound on his slumber fell
Than the lonesome tread of the sentinel —
    That equal, measured pace —
And the wind that came from the cracking pine,
And the dying oak, and the swinging vine,
In many a weary, weary line,
    To his pale and hollow face.

But the soldier slept, and his dreams were bright
As the rosy glow of his bridal-night,
    With the angel on his breast;
For he passed away from the wintry gloom
To the softened light of a distant room,
Where a cat sat purring upon the loom,
    And his weary heart was blest.

His children came, two blue-eyed girls,
With laughing lips and sunny curls,
    And cheeks of ruddy glow;
And the mother pale, but lovely now,
As when, upon her virgin brow
He proudly sealed his early vow,
    In summer, long ago.

But the *reveillé* wild, in the morning gray,
Startled the beautiful vision away,
    As a frightened bird in the night;
And it seemed to the soldier's misty brain
But the shrill *tattoo* that sounded again,
And he turned with a dull, uneasy pain,
    To the camp-fires' dying light.

HEART LESSONS.

I HAD no design in passing —
I was walking rather late —
I did not dream that ROSA GRAY
Was standing at the gate ;

And when the cloud passed over,
And the moon revealed her there,
With its ripple on her bosom
And its shimmer in her hair,

I was startled at the glory
And the suddenness of light,
That had silvered up the arches
Over all the aisles of night.

I had kept my passion hidden ;
I had held it deathly still
Through the vigor of my manhood,
Through the power of my will.

G

Oh, the pride in being master!
  Oh, the dread of being slave!
Better wear the crimson fever
  In a by-way to the grave.

Better hold it — hide it downward,
  Though the fibrous, vital man
From the inner heat's expansion
  Into baser metal ran.

Better feel the slowest fusion
  Of the being's finer parts,
Than to show the garish colors
  And the flame of common hearts.

But this sudden, white appearance
  At the gate of ROSA GRAY,
Drove my real nature backward —
  Drove my stronger self away.

Standing, queenly, where the moon-glow
  Brought its finish to her cheek,
Where the star-eyes saw her breast-swells
  At the boddice-margin break,

Some entire unknown sensation,
  From the heart's entangled wild,
Broke amain upon my life-strings,
  And o'erswept me as a child.

She was looking far to seaward,
   And her outline shone so clear
That she seemed a chiseled SILENCE,
   Cut from silver, leaning there.

And the near Egyptian Lily,
   Bending from its marble vase,
Might be fairer for her whiteness,
   Might be rarer for her grace.

She was looking far to seaward,
   And the moon-path, silver laid,
For the passage of her vision
   To the outer world, was made.

She was lost in dreamy poems
   To the ever verseful sea,
And the dimmest stars were nearer
   Than her soul was unto me.

I approached her like a coward;
   For the under-lying dew
Scarcely sparkled at my foot-fall
   In its noiseless passage through.

" ROSA GRAY," I said, and touched her
   From her meditative sleep —
" What of all this coral labor :
   Will it overcome the deep ?

"Mark you yonder reef, unbroken
　　Through the foam-line of its length:
Has this boundless spread of water,
　　Or the insect, greater strength?

"Mark you how the brine beats ever
　　Up the still and steadfast wall:
Do the spray-drops gather marble,
　　That they whiten as they fall?

"There are grottos, arches, towers,
　　Cities, islands building on:
Will not Time proclaim a triumph
　　When the Ocean shall be gone?

"Come, now, ROSA GRAY, and listen:
　　Once my heart was all a sea,
And the thought-ships furrowed o'er it,
　　Bringing treasures unto me;

"Fair white sails from isles of learning,
　　Bringing knowledge unto me;
I was master of its commerce,
　　I was monarch of the sea.

"I could feel the waves go outward,
　　And the wind-share cutting free
Through the white-enameled furrows
　　Of my great, expanding sea.

" You began your labor early
 In my heart-deeps, ROSA GRAY,
And my ships, and waves, and ocean,
 Long ago have passed away.

" So you fill me now, and sway me,
 With the cunning of your skill ;
I have neither force nor reason,
 I have neither way nor will.

" Speak me truthful words, O mistress ¡
 In this fever of my mood ;
Let my heart-valves force the chalice,
 Be it poison, down my blood ! "

You have seen a twig inclining,
 Where, the liquid crystal found,
Kept the murmur of its music
 In the alleys underground ;

So I thought to find her spirit,
 So I sought to catch her tone,
Where the magic of my circle
 Was the compass of her zone.

And ROSA GRAY looked outward
 Once again toward the waves,
And her eyes came o'er with pity
 As the dews come over leaves ;

6 *

And my own eyes burning in them,
   Burning through the glassy flow,
Saw her real being shrinking
   In the darkness far below.

Little need for her to utter,
   Little need for her to move —
Friend, I came not in the margin
   Of the shadow of her love.

Mark you, now, I 'm looking backward,
   Somewhat further than it seems,
Where the real things that met us
   Take the portraiture of dreams.

There was no design in passing —
   I repeat here what I said —
I but followed where the genius
   Of my meditation led.

It was well I came upon her
   In that mystic, latter noon,
When my heart gave off its burthen
   As the cloud went off the moon.

It was well to yield my purpose
   To the sway of impulse then ;
It was well to bring my greatness
   To the plane of common men.

It was meet that I, a beggar,
  Trailing ermine as a king,
In her real, regal presence
  Should appear the lower thing.

What is human pride and purpose
  But a passion at the most?
Men are haunted through ambition,
  And their vanity 's the ghost.

For the lessons and the knowledge
  That she gave me, ROSA GRAY,
I would cast the garnered learning
  Of a former life away.

And I mind me often, often,
  In my wanderings of late,
Of the figure standing silent
  In the halo at the gate.

And I tread the pathway backward,
  To that mystic, latter noon,
When my heart gave off its burthen
  As the cloud went off the moon.

TIME AT THE SOUTH.

In the shade of the pool, where the queen-lily dips,
With the dew of the night on her beautiful lips;

Where blossoms the orange, where bloometh the rose,
And the bright oleander and jessamine blows;

Tread lightly, tread softly, O merciful Time,
O'er the land of the sun, and the lemon, and lime;

For leaves of the flowers so faded and strewn
Were fair in the morning and fallen at noon.

Go back to the plane of your ice-hidden lakes —
Go back with your breath of the frost and the flakes;

Go Northward, O season of Winter and gloom,
From the emerald South and its odorous bloom.

O, the purple dead leaves that environ the ways
Of the genius of Time in its passage of days;

O, the late-fallen leaves and the withering grass —
How they rustle, and gather, and people the pass!

80

O, better to die and be hidden away,
Than to live in the circle and sight of decay.

Our metals of life in their crucibles run
When the pulses are red in the glow of the sun.

But come to the South with the ice of your heel,
And the channels are still and the currents congeal.

Go backward, O Winter, go back to the lakes,
With your withering frost and your wandering flakes.

* * * * * *

The bush is borne down and the blossom is shed,
And we gather to-day at the grave of the dead.

The corse that is stark, and the body that's cold,
Is a link of the past to be lost in the mold;

And armies may file to the sepulchre plain
To laurel the bier of the body that's slain;

But never again, at the death of the years,
Will the heart of the Southron be lavish of tears.

Go seek in the far-reaching fields of his land,
For the shade of his column and capital grand;

Go look for the mosque of his worship and pride;
Go look for his brother — go look for his bride;

Go look for all things he has cherished and loved—
The garden he haunted, the valley he roved —

And the desolate track, and the ravens that fly,
Will tell that the fount of the Southron is dry.

Time was, when a sentinel stood at the gate,
And guarded the annals and altars of state;

When the gleam of his eye and the glare of his blade
Kept the wolf in the covert afar and afraid;

When the good and the pure, and the noble and true,
Were all in the land that the sentinel knew:

Time was when the tyrant would blanch in the sight
Of the column and arch of our temple of right,

When the marbles. of state in their purity stood,
That our fathers had builded and hallowed in blood,

But time is long gone with the sands of the glass,
When *honor* was watchword, and *virtue* the pass.

Go banish the dust from your lexicons old,
Ye people that glitter and seek to be gold;

Go back to the schools of your earlier days,
For their lessons of truth, and their patriot lays,

Go study the greatness, that tried in the fires,
Shone bright in the glory that covered your sires;

Go feel in the spell that encircles their graves
That tyrants and cowards are meaner than slaves.

Oh, men of the nation — oh, rulers and kings,
Do ye know that your riches and powers have wings?

Do ye know that the ashes ye scatter and spurn,
Must quicken in time and arise from the urn?

Do ye know that the gates where ye gather your tolls,
Are peopled with things that have pulses and souls?

Do ye dare, from your source in the dust and the clods,
To covet the robes and the thrones of the gods?

Ye may look at the waves that go out on the sea,
And learn from the past what your future will be;

For the ocean is broad, and the wave in its track,
Must follow, and follow, and never come back.

Ye are like to the waves that are gathered and tost,
And driven to sea, to be scattered and lost —

In the morn, ere the scent of the roses is o'er,
Ye may sleep in the cove and the calm of the shore;

Ye may toy in the isles at the mellower noon,
With your feathery spray and its murmurous tune;

But evening must come from the shadow at last,
With a garment of gloom and a gathering blast.

DOUBLE LIFE.

Over pools of purest water,
  Lying silent, there will come,
Soon, or late, the green enamel
  Of a quickened herbage-scum;
Taking color from the vesture
  That the margin grasses wear,
Till it hides the lambent sparkle
  Of the liquid crystal there.

So the poet-nature shadows
  All its glory with a cloud,
That the soul-light may not dazzle
  In the ordinary crowd;
So they hide their real beings,
  So they live and act a part,
Making nature but an adjunct
  To the perfectness of art.

Oh, I hate this outward seeming,
  This unreal, double-life,

Where the face is full of quiet
  While the heart is full of strife ;
For our latent inner-currents
  Would to other currents run,
Though the waters of the spirit
  May be hidden from the sun.

We may live upon the surface,
  We may wear the mantle green,
And among the outer beings,
  Be as outer beings seen ;
But the spheres of souls magnetic
  Are beyond the common thrall,
And the true life of the poet
  Pulseth under, after all.

II

THE LITTLE BOY GUIDING THE PLOW.

When a bugle-note rang in the quivering trees,
  And a drum beat the nation to arms,
Our people came up from the shore of the seas,
  And away from their blue-mountain farms;
All stalwart and strong as the hardy old pines,
  Or the wave-breaking rocks of the shore,
They came in their long gleaming columns and lines,
  Till the bugle-note sounded no more.
There are hearts in the ranks, as light as the foam;
  There are those of a gloomier brow;
And some who have left but a mother at home,
  With her little boy guiding the plow.

There are silver-haired men, the tide in their veins
  Leaping down the red alleys of youth,
All fresh as the water-fall thrown to the plains,
  And as pure as the beautiful truth;
There are sons too, and sires — the old and the
      young —
  In the midnight and morning of life,
  86

Who came from the hills and the valleys among,
  To be first in the glorious strife;
And many, how many beneath the blue dome,
  Are bending in solitude now,
To plead for the weal of a mother at home,
  And her little boy guiding the plow!

Oh, the pang of his heart, and the keenest of all
  That a wandering father may know,
Is the vision of home with its agony-call,
  Its hunger and shivering woe;
And who would not chafe in the sacredest chain
  At a memory bitter as this,
Though he knew in his heart that each moment of
      pain
  Would but hallow his future to bliss?
And who would not weep in a vision of gloom,
  When the Evil One whispered him how
The toil grew apace to the mother at home,
  And her little boy guiding the plow?

But courage, keep courage, oh, parent away!
  Be noble, and faithful, and brave!
And the midnight shall pass, and the glorious day
  Shall be shed over tyranny's grave!
Though a desolate thing is a fenceless farm,
  And as dreary, a furrowless field,
Still, God in his mercy shall strengthen the arm
  Of the little boy asking a yield;

And the stubbornest clay shall be as the loam,
  When the patriot spirit shall bow,
And ask for a friend to the mother at home,
  And her little boy guiding the plow.

Oh, God will be kind to the needy and poor
  Who shall suffer from tyranny's hand;
His foot-print shall be by the loneliest door,
  And his bounty shall cover the land;
And broken the glebe in the valley and mead,
  Where the poorest and weakest shall be,
And plenty shall spring of the promising seed,
  Till a people shall live to be free;
And never, oh, never shall tyranny come,
  With iron-bound bosom and brow —
May God give him back to the mother at home,
  And her little boy guiding the plow!

THE FLOWER GRAVES.

From the fields that underlie us,
  Down the flowered South's incline,
Where the vintage of the battles
  Took a deeper glow than wine;
When the early green of summer,
  Winning out the smitten gaze,
Caught, from war, a sudden crimson,
  As of later autumn days;
Where the tangled, trodden grasses,
  And the fragment blades and shells,
All the story of the struggle,
  More than eloquently tells;

From the salients and the centres,
  And the points of jealous guard,
Where the trees and earth with missiles
  Bearing death were deepest scarred;
Where the tempered blade was needed,
  And the gallant arm to wield,
For the honor and the glory
  And the guidance of the field;

11 *

In the surge and edge of carnage,
   In the battle's tidal flow,
At the focus of the conflict,
   At the colors of the foe —
There we sought, and *there* we found them —
   In the clotted field and fen —
Found the relics, and the shadows,
   Of our grand and god-like men.

Meet it is, oh widow — mother ! —
   From this sweet, prolific May,
Thus to bear its living garlands
   Through the winter of your way.

Meet it is, O men and brothers !
   Here amid the fallen great,
These to glorify and honor
   As the noblest of your State.

In the shadow of a column,
   Bearing upward to the day,
Yonder carven marble semblance
   Of the ever-living CLAY,
Well it is that they should slumber,
   Who, beneath his power-tone,
From the cradle-time of being,
   Into patriots had grown ;
Who were early taught his lessons,
   And to noble paths inclined

By his scorn of crawling spirits,
　And the narrow grooves of mind ;
Who were taught the worth of freedom,
　And the glory of such graves
As should come before the shackles,
　And the curse of being slaves.

Bring your garlands here, O sister,
　For the brother who is free,
Who to brutal pomp and power
　Never bent a servile knee.

For the cause in which he suffered,
　And the hearth and home-lands gone,
Yet his ashes rise in witness
　At the courts of after-dawn —
Let his banner bear the record
　Of an impulse in his blade,
When the red track down an army
　Told the havoc he had made.

Such an even-handed justice
　As the nation's cannot move,
There will be in that tribunal,
　At the golden bar above.

Bring the rose and lily hither,
　And the May-time's early bloom ;
Let us conquer now, with flowers,
　All the legions of the tomb ;

Let the green and living garlands
    Over all the mounds be shed,
As a token that the heroes
    Underlying, are not dead.

Keep them fresh, O eyes of beauty,
    With the moisture of your tears,
That their souls may haunt the flowers
    Down your summer-way of years.
Keep them fresh with darling kisses;
    Let them feel your bosom-sigh,
And the thousand years of glory
    Shall not see the Southrons die.

FALLEN.

THE iron voice from yonder spire
  Has hush'd its hollow tone,
And midnight finds me lying here,
  In silence and alone.

The still moon through my window
  Sheds its soft light on the floor,
With a melancholy paleness,
  I have never seen before;

And the summer wind comes to me
  With its sad Æolian lay,
As if burthened with the sorrows
  Of a weary, weary day;

But the moonlight cannot soothe me
  Of the sickness here within,
And the sad wind takes no portion
  From my bosom's weight of sin.

Yet my heart and all its pulses
   Seem so quietly to rest,
That I scarce can feel them beating
   In my arms, or in my breast:

These rounded limbs are resting now
   So still upon the bed,
That one would think, to see me here,
   That I was lying dead.

What if 'twere so? What if I died
   As I am lying now,
With something like to virtue's calm
   Upon this pallid brow?

What if I died to-night? Ah, now
   This heart begins to beat —
A fallen wretch, like me, to pass
   From earth, so sadly sweet!

Yet am I calm! — as calm as clouds
   That slowly float and form,
To give their burthen-tears in some
   Unpitying winter storm;

As calm as great Sahara
   E'er the simoom sweeps its waste —
As the ocean, e'er the billows
   All its miles of beach have laced.

Still, still, I have no tears to shed;
  These eye-lids have no store —
The fountain once within me,
  A fountain is no more.

The moon alone looks on me now,
  The pale and dreamful moon;
She smiles upon my wretchedness,
  Through all the night's sweet noon.

What if I died to-night — within
  These gilded, wretched walls,
Upon whose crimson tapestry
  No eye of virtue falls.

What would its soulless inmates do
  When they had found me here,
With cheek too white for passion's smile,
  Too cold for passion's tear?

Ah! one would come, and from these arms
  Unclasp the bauble bands;
Another, wrench the jewels from
  My fairer, whiter hands.

This splendid robe, another's form
  Would grace, oh, long before
The tender moon-beam shed again
  Its silver on the floor.

And when they'd laid me down in earth
　　Where pauper graves are made,
Beneath no drooping willow-tree
　　In angel-haunted shade,

Who'd come and plant a living vine
　　Upon a wretched grave?
Who'd trim the tangled grasses wild
　　No summer wind could wave?

Who would raise a stone to mark it
　　From ruder graves around,
That the foot-fall of the stranger
　　Might be soft upon the ground?

No stone would stand above me there —
　　No sadly bending tree,
No hand would plant a myrtle vine
　　Above a wretch like me.

What if I died to-night! — and when
　　To-morrow's sun had crept
Where late the softer moonlight
　　In its virgin beauty slept,

They'd come and find me here — oh, who
　　Would weep to see me dead?
Who'd bend the knee of sorrow
　　By a pulseless wanton's bed?

There's one would come — *my mother!*
  God bless the angel band
That bore her, ere her daughter fell,
  To yonder quiet land!

Thank God for all the anthem-songs
  That gladdened angels sung,
When my mother went to heaven,
  And I was pure and young!

And there's another too would come —
  A man upon whose brow
My shame hath brought the winter snow
  To rest so heavy now.

Ah! he would come with bitter tears
  All burning down his cheek,—
Had *reason's* kingdom stronger been
  When *virtue* grew so weak!

My sisters and my brothers all,
  Thank God! are far away!
They'll never know how died the one
  That mingled in their play;

They'll never know how wretchedly
  Their darling sister died,
The one who smiled whene'er they smiled,
  Who cried whene'er they cried.

I

For him that sought a spotless hand,
  And lives to know my shame,
In such a place I'd tear the tongue
  That dared to speak his name.

The cold sea-waves run up the sand
  In undulating swells,
And backward to the ocean turn
  When they have kissed the shells;

So, there's a torrent in my breast,
  And I can feel its flow
Rush up in crimson billows
  On a beach as fair as snow;

And backward, backward to my heart,
  The ocean takes its tide,
My cheeks and lips left bloodless all,
  And cold, as if I died!

I'm all alone to-night! How strange
  That I should be alone!
This splendid chamber seems to want
  Some *roué's* passion-tone!

Yon soulless mirror, with its smooth
  And all untarnished face,
Sees not these jewelled arms to-night,
  In their unchaste embrace —

Oh, I have fled the fever
Of that heated, crowded hall,
Where I might claim the highest-born
And noblest of them all ;

Where I might smile upon them now
With easy, wanton grace,
Which subdues the blood of virtue
That would struggle in my face.

I hate them all — I scorn them,
As they scorn me in the street ;
I could spurn away the pressure
That my lips too often meet ;

I could trample on the lucre
That their passion never spares :
They robbed me of a heritage
Of greater price than theirs.

They can never give me back again
What I have thrown away,
The brightest jewel woman wears
Throughout her little day !

The brightest, and the only one,
That from the cluster riven,
Shuts out forever woman's heart
From all its hopes of Heaven !

What if I died to-night? — and died
  As I am lying here!
There's many a green leaf withered
  Ere autumn comes to sear;

There's many a dew-drop shaken down
  Ere yet the sunshine came,
And many a spark hath died before
  It wakened into flame.

What if I died to-night, and left
  These wretched bonds of clay
To seek beyond this hollow sphere
  A brighter, better day?

What if my soul passed out, and sought
  That haven of the blest
"Where the wicked cease from troubling,
  The weary are at rest"?

Would angels call me from above,
  And beckon me to come
And join them in their holy songs
  In that eternal home?

Would they clasp their hands in gladness
  When they saw my soul set free,
And point—beside my mother's —
  To a place reserved for me?

Would they meet me as a sister,
  As one of precious worth
Who had gained a place in Heaven
  By holiness on earth?

O God! I would not have my soul
  Go out upon the air
With all its weight of wretchedness,
  To wander, where — oh, where?

I *

MIDNIGHT BELLS.

Ho! ye who wait where sleeps in state
The silent form of SIXTY-EIGHT,
Where from the shadows blue and far
Has come his glinting taper-star,
Where from the carboned upper dark
The crystal scalings of its arc,
In fitful, hither, thither ways,
Are driven like the drifting days,—
Now o'er the winter fields and fells
Ye hear the sobbing Midnight Bells.

Ho! ye whose tears were shed on biers
Of other gray and gathered years,
Why weep ye now, and watch, and wait,
Beside the corse of SIXTY-EIGHT?
The widowed hills, the orphan vales,
May give their anthems and their wails;
May wear their garb of mourning white
Along the pathways of the night,—
But YE! why heed ye now the knells?
Why hearken still the Midnight Bells?

The sunlight smiles through airy miles
On fair and flowered summer isles,
And earth in green and living things,
So gladdened with its lightsome wings,
Floats wanton where the odor-breeze
Goes out the shining summer seas;
But winter from her secret caves
Creeps darkling o'er the ocean waves,
And sad and far from o'er the swells
The bloom has heard its Midnight Bells.

O men who know how sure and slow
The tides of time must ebb and flow;
How one by one the waves must reach
And bear their tribute from the beach,
How sure the sands upon the lea
Go outward to the central sea,
And buried are in hollow grooves
Where slow th' eternal current moves,—
Why pause they where the sounding shells
Bear echoes from the Midnight Bells?

The nations rise, and through the skies
The clamor of their glory flies;
Their flaunting pennons out the gales
Go with the sunlight and the sails,
And spicy isles and frozen zones
Their splendor and their power owns;
But deathless Time — eternal TIME!
He heeds no king, he knows no clime;

And over wars, their shouts, their yells,
He peals the nations' Midnight Bells.

The great, the grand, who gave the land
Their crimson for its right to stand;
Who on their swords of valor brought
Our right of action and of thought;
Who piled their way from kings and thrones
With such a hecatomb of bones,—
Their hearts are still, their forms are cold,
Their very deeds beneath the mold,
And scarce the country's record tells
How we have heard their Midnight Bells.

When tyrant knaves make freemen slaves,
And tread the sod of sacred graves;
When in the darkness and the dust
They give our sabres to the rust;
When in our cells no sound remains
Above the voices of the chains;
When all but memory is dead,
And TIME alone hath ceaseless tread,—
Oh, joy to know a chain foretells
The clanking of their Midnight Bells!

For men whose souls amid the shoals
Are fearless in the tidal rolls;
Who move with shackles on their arms
As proudly in the face of storms

As they whose ermine drapes the gates
Of conquered Empires, fallen States,—
To them shall come no craven gloom,
No haunting shadow of the tomb,
No fear of death, no shrieking hells,
When Freedom swings her Midnight Bells.

The fairest stream that like a dream
Goes down the land, a silver seam;
The stars that show their golden glow
On things that slumber here below;
The waves, the sea, the earth, the sky,
All things that live and all that die;
The great, the good, the weak, the strong,—
To TIME ETERNAL all belong,
And soon or late must come their knells
From sad and solemn Midnight Bells.

In virtue's way to endless day,
Beyond the margin's reaching gray,
Beyond the ether's thick'ning spread,
Beyond the world, beyond the dead,—
Let men, let nations cast their eyes
Toward the opening Paradise,
Till all the hopes and all the fears,
Till all the chains and all the wars
Are lost forever in the swells
When Heaven tolls our Midnight Bells.

AFTER THE WAR.

WE have filled with recollections
   All our calumets to-day,
And from this clearer present
   Floats the cloudy past away.

We have burned to finer ashes
   All the *débris* of the years,
That so late amid the home-lands
   Brought us misery and tears.

Farewell to all the memories
   That preyed upon our souls,
That made us in our carnage-time
   A populace of ghouls.

Farewell to every record-mark
   Of cruelties and crimes,
And a welcome to the sunlights
   Of dawning better times.

Already from the havoc-fields
  Where rolled the battle-drums,
The busy beat of hammers
  And the din of labor comes;

The plowshare in the sodden ground
  Its fruitful passage takes,
And toil is in its triumph
  From the bayous to the lakes.

O blessed land! where swords are drawn
  To hew the armied grain,
Where lines of corn are stricken down
  Upon the harvest plain;

Where every stalk beneath the stroke
  In golden beauty bows,
And men are counted noble
  Who have sweat upon their brows.

O blessed land! O land of toil,
  And land of human love,
There are pages of repentance
  In thy records up above;

And onward, onward through the days
  Of glory yet to come
Shall march thy legion labor,
  Shall beat their anvil-drum.

Our sinews strong from North to South
    Are wrought of iron bands,
And rivers wind like silver threads
    Adown our shining sands.

Brave Progress with her certain pulse,
    Her mighty breath of steam,
Goes out in power on the earth,
    In glory on the stream.

And Westward far, by plains a-bloom
    And mountains rich in ore,
Our engines bear their burthens
    To the great Pacific shore.

Our sails are white on all the seas,
    With gleaming tracks behind —
At peace to-day with all the world!
    Good-will to all mankind!

Thus much for all the nation
    As a grand majestic whole,
Made up of smaller portions
    As our acts make up the soul.

God hath trusted us with talents,
    Each and all of us a trust;
Howsoe'er we please to use them,
    He is merciful and just.

Let us do our share of labor,
　Let us toil and sweat to-day,
Let us lift our burthened neighbor
　From his falling by the way.

Every impulse of our kindness,
　Every act we do of love,
Hath its record to our credit
　In the archives up above.

*　　*　　*　　*　　*　　*

By the broad and fair Ohio,
　In the rich lands of the West,
We have builded up our mansions,
　Here to live and here to rest;

And the long grass waves in greenness
　Over plains and over hills,
And the sunlight gives its shimmer
　To the ever-going rills.

Land of Peace and land of Plenty!
　Richer far than any yet:
May thy rising sun of glory
　In the shadow never set!

Goodly arms and sturdy spirits
　Over all thy fields be spread;
Teach the children of thy people
　To be proud to earn their bread!

J

Never plowman trod the furrow
  Of a richer soil than ours,
To a bosom more prolific
  Never came the summer showers;

Corn and wheat in rolling billows
  Flood the acres with their gold,
And the strata spreading under
  Have a hidden wealth untold.

Build the lordly track of iron
  Through the pasture-lands and fields,
That its greater strength may gather in
  And garner up the yields;

Let the palpitating engines
  Spread their steam adown the valleys,
And the woodlands hanging over
  Keep its echo in their alleys.

Send the golden harvest outward,
  Bear away the corn and kine;
Open up the secret treasure
  Of the underlying mine;

Show the world your share of riches,
  Give to commerce what you can;
Show the dignity of labor
  And the worthiness of man!

SIXTY-FIVE

IF a nation hath not goodness then it never can be
　　great,
For there's nothing like to virtue in the building of
　　a State.
Though you bring your quarried marble from a mul-
　　titude of miles,
And rear it into palaces and monumental piles ;
Though with dome and arch and column you may
　　beautify the land,
Making earth and air and water pliant agents in your
　　hand,
Still without the seal of virtue on the charter of your
　　State,
In the eyes of Christian people you are neither good
　　nor great ;
In the eyes of God Almighty you are only great in
　　sin,
And he'll weigh you in the autumn when His Angel
　　garners in.

Let us look a moment calmly o'er the little season
    gone ;
Let us mark the boggy places in the road we journey
    on :
There are others to come after in the path which we
    have trod,
Let us point them from the quicksand to the way
    upon the sod.

There were mighty throes upon us when we ushered
    in the year
Which yesterday in solemn shroud we saw upon its
    bier ;
There were throes as if a giant on our being bent a
    knee,
Admonishing of what we were and what we sought
    to be ;
We had coffers heavy laden, we had ships upon the
    brine,
We had fallow-lands and vineyards with their effer-
    vescing wine ;
We were strong and stern and haughty from the
    growth of years before,
And our plenitude of glory only made us crave the
    more :
Not such glory as the Christian, in the presence of
    his God,
Hath to come upon his spirit when he bows to kiss
    the rod ;
But the vanity of power and the strength of human
    pride,

That had made us scorn the virtues and the honors
    as they died :
So a hand was laid upon us, and our glory stripped
    away
As one might strip a flower-stem upon an autumn
    day.

We have conquered many battles, we have gained a
    world-renown,
We have driven gallant armies and have shaken cities
    down ;
We have laid a land in ashes, we have made a people
    slaves,
We have carried golden trophies from a citadel of
    graves ;
There's blood upon our bayonets and blood upon
    our guns,
And some of it's our brothers' blood and some of
    it's our sons'.
"What boots it how we triumphed so a victory was
    gained !
Who wears the whiter garment may expect to have
    it stained !"
Thus spoke we in our vanity, our ecstasy of pride,
As one who goes rejoicing o'er the grave of one that
    died ;
So climbed we up the pathway to the pinnacle of
    sin,
And o'er the gulf of darkness we were calmly look-
    ing in.

But the wrath of God was on us, and we felt His
    mighty hand
As he stripped the mad ambition of its garments in
    the land.
We were "proud and strong and haughty," but within
    a little day
We have seen our gilded treasures fast as bubbles
    float away:
We are wrecked in pride and fortune; we were rich,
    and we are poor;
There's a coffin in our dwelling and a sexton at our
    door.

Let us turn the crimson pages in the record-book of
    war:
There are giant sins upon us, giant crimes to answer
    for:
There are cities laid in ashes, there are desolated
    farms;
There are starving children crying in their helpless
    mother's arms;
There are widows, there are orphans, cold and home-
    less in the land,
With the husband and the father lying fleshless on
    the sand;
There is woe and want and sorrow over all the South-
    ern States;
From within the nation's chamber, we can hear it at
    the gates;
Yet our flags are flaunting bravely, and our music
    fills the air,

For the burthen of the sorrow it is not for us to
  bear ;
We have prison-cells and dungeons thickly peopled
  with the foe,
And some have on the gibbet died, and some are
  dying slow.

Such a fever and such passion over all the North
  has swept,
That though weeping MERCY pleaded, it hath never
  known she wept ;
And the vengeful cry for slaughter from the Puri-
  tanic crowd,
In the halls of central power hath an echo fierce
  and loud ;
From the Northern press and pulpit, from the bench
  and from the bar,
Cometh all the evil pleading of a fury after war.
And but a little while it seems, when frenzy ran so
  high
The nation by a gallows stood to see a woman die—
A woman weak and trembling and as guiltless as a
  child,
But a victim to the fury of a passion fierce and wild.
And here the high offended God put forth His hand
  again,
To write upon the nation's brow the burning mark
  of CAIN.
Again for WIRZ, the foreigner, a wretched feeble man,
But yesterday we filled his cup until it over-ran ;

And one by one we lessen them, these victims to our
    hate,
And there's a thirst for human blood an ocean can
    not sate.

At our helm we had a despot, and for him this crim-
    son tide,
A Nero who could revel while his better subjects
    died ;
But the Mighty Hand o'ertook him in his revel and
    his wrong,
And it taught us in our weakness that the Deity
    was strong.
There are those who call him martyr, there are those
    who call him great:
After *passion* cometh *reason* — let the better spirits
    wait ;
As the water finds its level, so the characters of men—
Some may die and be forgotten, some may die and
    live again.
There's a gray-haired man in prison, under iron bolt
    and bar,
A relic and a trophy from the desolating war ;
He was once a mighty leader, such as few are born
    to be ;
He had armies in the nation, he had ships upon the
    sea ;
But our strength in war was greater, for we crushed
    him with our might,
And we watched his day of glory as it settled into
    night.

Now we hold him bound and shackled, with a palsy
    in his arm ;
We have seized and sacked his temple, he is power-
    less for harm.
But to crush and break his spirit, and to take away
    his all,
For the crime of Revolution was a punishment too
    small ;
And the nation must have vengeance, for her women
    cry for blood—
Though it runs a mighty torrent they would have it
    run a flood.
God forgive them all their passion ! God forgive them
    all their sin !
From their hearts drive out the anger, and invoke the
    mercy in !

There's another cry of sorrow from the liberated
    black ;
There is want among his children, and blood upon
    his track.
From his proper grade and level they have thought
    to lift him up,
And he glories at their banquet with a poison in his
    cup.
From his love and from his labor they have taken
    him away,
And the gloomy night is crowding over all his sunny
    day.
We can hear him in the darkness giving out his bit-
    ter moan,

While for all the bread he asketh they have only
    found a *stone.*
Let him freeze and let him hunger—they are blind
    and cannot see;
It is food and cloth and shelter, and a glory to be
    FREE.
O ye great and godly Christians! O ye Puritanic
    souls,
Have ye lost your human spirits? are ye demons?
    are ye ghouls?
Was it not enough to wreck him in his hopes and in
    his all,
That ye triumph so and revel at his miserable fall?

Though the sins of all the nation in their multitude
    are great,
There are crimes as black and cruel in the records
    of our State;
For Kentucky (God forgive her), though she sought
    to do the best,
From the black and base attrition grew as callous
    as the rest.
There were those who did her murder in the guise
    of right and law;
There's the blood of HUNT upon her, and of CORBIN
    and McGRAW;
And there's such a cry of sorrow from the grave of
    bleeding LONG,
As should pale the cheek of hatred in its memory of
    the wrong.

     *   *   *   *   *   *

God forgive us all our errors! God forgive us all our
    crimes !
We have lived in sin and darkness — let us hope for
    better times.

TO MASTER GEO. W. JOHNSTON.

In youth, my boy, I pray you keep
This simple truth in view:
That men are only counted great
For goodly things they do.

The man who lives an aimless life,
Nor labors every day,
Belongs to that ephemera
That passes soon away;

But he who takes the labor-tools
And seeks the science-fields,
Will find the noble harvest that
The golden autumn yields.

The way to fame is over-grown
With tangled weeds and vines,
And many take the trodden path
That from the goal inclines;

But you, my boy, with compass true,
  Must keep the bearing straight,
And cut the stubborn obstacles
  That lie before the gate.

Be guided by the honor-laws
  That gave your kindred name,
And keep the course that ushered them
  Within the walls of fame ;

And when at last the honor-roll
  Above the world is spread,
You will not blush to find your name
  Is written at the head.

K

HIS LAST DAY.

As one who from his native place
　In tender youth had turned,
To feel the brown upon his face
　By distant solstice burned ;
Who, journey-worn and scarred and sore,
　And sickened with the past,
Has reached again his father's door,
　And tottered in at last ;

As one whose memory at home
　Is slowly fading out,
Whose features to his kindred come
　In mistiness and doubt ;
Who from the sea has turned again
　The ingle-side to share,
And fled the haunts of stranger men
　To be a stranger *there*.

So I, to-night, a loiterer
　In other paths and lands,

From struggle-scenes and wreck and fear,
  And *death* upon the sands,
Have turned again an eager gaze
  Upon the homeward track,
And through the mist and through the maze
  Have slowly travelled back.

Here home at last! ah, HOME no more!
  For time hath hurtled through,
And faces that I study o'er,
  Alas! are strange and new;
All new! all strange, save only one,
  The old Familiar there;
And Time his silver-work hath done
  Upon the master's hair.

I keep the outline of his face
  As faithfully of late,
As when with early artist-grace
  I "did him" on the slate:
The kindly eye, the open brow,
  The lips that ever smiled,
I mark them just as truly now
  As when I was a child.

The bold front teeth, the queer-turned nose
  (Your pardon, sir, I pray),
The forward step upon the toes,
  They seem like yesterday.

Though Time hath fled with gray and brown,
  I mark him just as well
As when he pulled the old rope down
  And tied me to the bell.

Full thirty years have fleeted by
  Since first the school began,
And from a little urchin I
  Have grown to be a man ;
But I would dash the cares of men
  And give — I cannot tell —
If he could take me back again
  And tie me to the bell.

The dear companions of my class,
  Habitués at play,
Have some of them gone down the glass,
  And some live *great* to-day.
I've watched the progress of them all,
  And in the ways of fame
I hear at every honor-call
  Some well-remembered name.

The pulpit and the bench and bar,
  The science-fields of earth,
The blood-red annals of the war
  Are vocal with their worth.
Throughout the land, from East to West,
  From Erie to the Keys,
The spirits known and loved the best
  Were nurtured here — like these.

When late, for sad fraternal strife
  Our battle lines were drawn,
And North and South alike were rife
  With armies marching on,
A portion of the early class
  On either side were found ;
And some are 'neath the trampled grass,
  And some live yet renowned.

All honor to the dust of those
  Who in the struggle fell,
Who grew as friends but met as foes,
  And fought each other well ;
Their soldier-graves shall long attest
  To future passers-by,
That *dulce et decorum est*
  Pro patria mori.

I come to-night with weary heart
  And saddened eye, to find
Some vestige of the scholar-art
  Left years ago behind :
The labors of the early age,
  The mysteries of school,
The art to scan a Virgil page,
  The Algebraic rule.

From other scenes and other toils
  Too late, alas ! I turn ;
    K *

The science-lamps their sacred oils
   No more for me shall burn.
The springs of youth that joyous sped
   Their courses to the river,
Have mingled with the waves, and fled
   The flower-ways forever.

What though a stranger in the throng
   That now the master sways,
I claim the right to give my song
   The flush of other days ;
And here upon this honored stand
   A gratitude to show
To him who gave a guiding hand,
   So many years ago.

Ah, more than all, to-night should band
   The early friends and true,
To take the master's honest hand,
   And bid him here adieu ;
Nay, let the gush of tender years
   Adown their channels run ;
The labor of his thirty years
   Is well and nobly done.

ELMWOOD.

I, ALONE of all at Elmwood —
　I, alone of all,
Hear the night-sands dropping slowly,
　Hear them as they fall.
Over me the spirit's slumber
　That these moments bring,
Has not cast the sombre shadow
　Of the night's narcotic wing.

Wakeful now, and full of feeling
　As the stars of light,
I can count the even-pulses
　Beating through the night;
I can count the palpitations
　Of the vision-driven hearts,
By the great magnetic power
　Which poetic night imparts.

There is one of all at Elmwood,
　One alone of all,

Who would start to know her pulses
 Echoed up the hall—
Echoed up the gloomy stairway
 And along the quiet hall—
One who in the glaring day-time
 Never beats a pulse at all.

Oh I read her, now she sleepeth;
 Feast upon her dream;
Catch the *real* of her spirit
 In its glory-beam.

We are strangers at the noontide;
 She a study deep to me,
She a language dead, a scripture
 Upon tablets in the sea.
But I read her now at midnight—
 Read her very soul;
Oh, I creep upon her slumber
 Silent as a ghoul;
And I feast upon her vision—
 Feast upon it, at the price
Which gave Adam wondrous knowledge,
 Whilst it lost him—Paradise!

RESPONSE—IMPROMPTU.

I DO not forget you—I never have thought
  A moment to check the sweet flow of our love;
I cannot forget what so lately you taught,
  I cannot throw down the bright wreath that you
    wove.

Oh the young bird of Hope, with its plumage of truth,
  That flits in the noontide of life's early spring,
Hath a season so brief in the gardens of youth
  That flowers but once feel the rush of its wing.

Not so when the sun has passed over the hill,
  To the autumn of life with its yellower sheaves;
If Hope comes at all, Oh its melodies fill
  In the long afternoon all the murmuring leaves.

I do not forget you—no, no! while my heart
  Hath been touched with the shadow of seasons
    gone by,

While lamp after lamp hath gone out at the start,
  I cannot believe that all passions will die.

I pray you forego every thought that would give
  But a color of falsehood to what I have said ;
'Twere shame that a spirit so faithless should live —
  'Twere better a friendship so hollow were dead.

Then let us strike hands in that honester way
  That tells to ourselves we are unriven friends ;
So when life shall have come to its twilight and
      gray,
  We may smile at the silvery thread that it sends.

BEAUTY.

She's not what you would simply call a woman,
A *thing* for this poor world's possession ;
There's something in her beauty more than human,
And far beyond expression.

Most woman-kind are only like the flowers
That blow at noon to wither at the gloaming ;
But she shall wander down my latest hours,
And be forever blooming.

131

TO KATY.

DEAR KATY, while I bless the hour
   That brings thine image up,
As fondly as some heated flower
   The dew-drop in its cup,
I backward turn my aching eyes,
   Through long and weary years,
To those who hear my saddest sighs,
   Who claim my sacred tears.

I greet thee as an angel fair
   Come by my gloomy hearth,
A thing divine, a spirit rare,
   An excellence on earth.
I love thee, Katy, for thy smile
   Shed o'er my frowning sky,
As sunlight through the dreary aisle
   I'm moving down to die.

For thee my lips with joyous words
   Should ever laden be,

Whilst thou wilt touch the music-chords
　To happy tunes for me ;
But, ah ! dissemble how I can,
　There is no pathic art
To stay the early tide that ran
　All riot in my heart.

To her upon whose gentle breast
　My little children sleep,
My soul goes ever back to rest,
　To worship and to weep ;
And backward, backward, through the years
　Of sorrow I have known,
My heart still wanders on to hers,
　Mine only and mine own.

Dear Katy, when thy winsome eye
　Hath wooed me down the lawn,
I could not always tell thee why
　My happy thoughts were gone ;
But thou, an angel in my way,
　A spirit by my side,
Forgav'st the burthened mind astray
　With hopes that early died.

Oh bless thee for thy kindly care,
　Oh bless thee for thy smile !
May Heaven greet thy virtues rare
　Beyond this world of guile ;
And when from joy and sorrow here
　Thy path is at the sea,
May such sweet flowers strew thy bier
　As thou hast thrown on me !

L

SECOND MARRIAGE.

THROW back the bright tresses that shadow thy brow,
  And let it look sunny and free ;
The flowers are blooming to circle it now,
  And a summer time opening to thee.

Thou hast felt the chill blast of a long winter's day,
  Whilst the stream in thy heart hath run 'cold ;
But the ice-frozen fetters are melting away,
  And the story of winter is told.

Oh let not a tear for the slumbering past
  Bedim the bright star in thine eye,
But cherish the gleam that hath wakened at last
  From its sleep on a lovelier sky.

There still is a chord in the lute of thy heart
  That sorrow has never swept o'er,
And gently and sweetly its music will start
  By the stream that is frozen no more.

134

MIDNIGHT AT SALT-SULPHUR.

With a snow-covered earth and a star-hidden sky,
Here is splendor enough for the wantonest eye.

Far up on the mountain the crystalline trees
Are still in the pause of the musical breeze,
And the wandering limbs intermingle above,
As clinging together in passionate love.

The erst-frowning rocks in a virginal white,
Bereft of their shadow, are smiling in night:
And the fair little stream, with its mystical flow,
Looks a silvery thread on a garment of snow.

A spirit might come from its region of bliss,
To stray in a midnight as lovely as this.

Could I brush every vestige of earth from my brow,
And die in a night-time as witching as now,
Oh, a moment of life in that beautiful sky
Were worth every pang it would give me to die.

SMOKE-PICTURES.

I sit at my window this sweet Sabbath even,
More bent upon earth than intent upon Heaven,
And trace the cloud-pictures that, floating afar,
Have gone at a breath from my fragrant cigar.

I catch through the smoke as it wantons away,
Like mist on the mountain-top scattered at day,
A glimpse here and there of the vistas and groves
Where youth flitted by with its passions and loves.

All green are the leaves, and as pleasantly still
I feel the wood-zephyrs abroad on the hill;
The vines reach above and the branches enwreathe,
While shadows fall soft on the verdure beneath.

No tinge of the autumn, no blight of the fall,
But summer, sweet summer, is over it all.

Oh, I fancy sometimes as I muse in the gloom,
With a friendly cigar to enrapture the room,

That winters may thicken and over me throw
Their garments as white as the silvery snow,
And dull to my eyes may the flowers appear
When woman-like summer embraces the year,
When birds in the branches with winningest strain
Would waken my soul to the music in vain;
That age with its chillest and woefulest way
May come to my heart in my life's latter day,
And Time, the remorseless, may beckon me on
Through ways where the weakest and oldest have
       gone —
As downward I tread to the brink of the river,
Whose waters flow silent forever and ever,
Still, still to my eye, though its vision be dark,
These pictures of youth shall pass out as an ark;
And o'er the sad waves of the Stygian stream
The sun of my Past shall so ardently beam,
That not the still tide in its passage of gloom,
Nor yet the cold brink where I look in my tomb,
Can fright me away from the memory dear
Of loves never dead and of leaves never sere;
But still in the light of my dream-haunted eyes,
These visions of youth shall forever arise;
For I cherish the pleasures that come from afar
To the vaporous smoke of my dreamy cigar.

CURE FOR HEADACHE.

My brain is athrob with a pulsing unrest,
 And fever is over my breath ;
Oh, bury my head in the snow of your breast,
 And let me be frozen to death.

138

UNDERNEATH.

Some tuneful words that in our hearts
  Bisect the prosy courses,
Do, by their rhythm, drive the parts
  Insensibly to verses.

While sadder things the autumn days
  Our outer lives are bringing,
A thousand summer roundelays
  The inner voice is singing.

What though we move in sober coats
  The Quaker masses after?
There's something welling in our throats,
  Unorthodox as laughter.

We take the sacerdotal stole
  And priestly surplice o'er us,

To hide the real music-soul
    And smother down its chorus.

What foolish arts beset us all !
    How we ourselves are tasking !
There's every day a funeral,
    And all the mourners masking.

SIXTY-SIX.

PROLOGUE.

THERE's a sculptor for the marbles
  Over all the buried years,
And his smooth and polished labor
  In a line of white appears.

He hath cunning with the chisel,
  And hath graved the record in,
Telling what the years departed
  In their living-time have been.

He has now a greater labor,
  Worthy all his better skill;
He has carved us many virtues —
  Let him carve us now the ILL.

From the black Egyptian marble
  Let him build a column high,
That the coming years may mark it
  In their quiet passage by.

Never yet hath sculptor graven
   More of crime or more of sin,
Than is better now for speaking
   What this latter year hath been!

We are moving slowly onward
   Through a vista-way of years;
We are looking to a future
   Full of sorrow and of tears;

There is not a light to guide us,
   Not a gleam upon the sky;
All our hopes are dead and buried,
   All our joys have flitted by.

We are not the Christian nation
   That we once were thought to be,
When with common voice we worshipped
   "From the centre to the sea."

We are not a godly people;
   We are very far away
From the path that leadeth outward
   To the everlasting day.

Let us see how much of virtue
   We have left in all the store,
Where a world hath looked and wondered
   In the happy days before.

Let us see how great and godly
　Are the acts of those who take
On themselves the nation's ermine
　For the troubled nation's sake.

First of all, we dare be tyrant —
　We who thought the English sway
Over torn and trampled Erin
　Should be rudely dashed away;

We who wept for bleeding Poland,
　And our Christian flag unfurled,
That its folds might flaunt defiance
　Unto al! a tyrant world.

We have learned another lesson
　In the onward march of time,
And we build our greatest virtue
　From the fabric of a crime;

And we spurn aside the maxim
　That "your truer blood will show;"
That "he is most ignoble
　Who would trample on a foe."

＊　　＊　　＊　　＊　　＊　　＊

We have swept our foreign legions
　Over all the Southern bands —
They were fewer than the Spartans,
　We were many as the sands —

And because of all their courage,
   All their stubbornness in fight,
All their pride of birth and section,
   All their love of human right,

We must put our feet upon them —
   We must crush and bend them low,
Test their better blood and breeding
   In the future "come to show."

This is Christian, this is proper,
   This is Puritanic law,
And we see the goodly future
   As our Plymouth fathers saw.

What are *they* that we should love them?
   They are little of our kin;
Seldom yet hath Southern current
   Let the Northern current in.

Proud of blood and proud of bearing,
   Quick in anger to a foe,
Never yet hath given insult
   Been without attendant blow.

We are calmer, better balanced,
   We are cooler in our veins;
We have less of heart in battle,
   More of calculating brains;

We are not a kindred people,
    And the passage yet of years
Will not mix the Plymouth waters
    With the blood of Cavaliers!

Next, we claim a godly power,
    And we widen out our span
When we raise the apish negro
    To the standard of a man.

This we do for godly reasons —
    Such our early fathers gave,
"That the servant may be master,
    And the master may be slave."

Thus we raise him from the level
    To his greatest earthly goal,
And we take away his instinct,
    And we give him back a soul —

Such a soul as we are given,
    Such a soul as makes him great:
He is worthy of the chancel,
    He is worthy of the State!

He may come into our circles,
    He may mingle with our blood,
He shall be our equal brother
    As he was before the Flood.

M

Though the curse of God was on him,
　　Though he wandered in the land,
We would give him whitest vesture,
　　We would take him by the hand.

In the summer all our meadows
　　Were a-bloom with scented hay,
And the corn upon our acres
　　Spread its fullness far away;

All the shadows of the woodland
　　Were astir with heavy kine,
And the hill-sides gave their treasure
　　From the rich Catawba vine.

Far indeed from cold and hunger,
　　Far indeed from want and woe,
We are in the golden current,
　　In the glory of its flow.

Let the people down below us,
　　In the desolated land,
Starve and shiver in the palaces
　　They built upon the sand;

We have corn and wine and vesture—
　　Let it rot and let it mould;
They have nothing now to give us,
　　Neither human love nor gold.

O ye rich and pampered people!
O ye cold and cruel men!
They have crossed your swords in battle,
They were one and you were ten!

Dare you press your heel upon them,
When ye usher back the day
That your full and feasted legions
Fled before the starving *Grey?*

Are ye cowards, are ye cravens
That ye fear to let them live?
Can ye see a nation perish
Whilst ye have the food to give?

They had richer fields and vineyards,
Better homes and broader lands,
Till ye threw the torch among them
From your desolating bands.

They were proof against your valor,
They had better-tempered steel —
Think ye now your servant Hunger
Will be proud to see them kneel.

Not to you, O callous stranger!
Not to baser blood and birth
Will the true chivalric Southron
Bend his knee upon the earth.

Better starve amid the ruins
   Of his fallen arch and dome!
Better die amid the ashes
   Of his violated home!

Not for cold nor not for hunger
   Will he kiss your iron rod:
There's an altar for his kneeling,
   It is only to his God!

What of him who, great and noble,
   Stood so very long at bay,
Whilst the veterans drawn around him
   Left their crimson in the way?

Still in bondage, still in prison,
   Living still yet near to death,
Never yet hath human being
   Drawn on earth a prouder breath

First among his race and kindred,
   First among his noble clan,
He has taught a cruel nation
   How to suffer as a man.

All that cunning, all that malice,
   All that human hate can do,
All that any Christian martyr
   In his dying ever knew,

He has known and felt and suffered,
  And his spirit liveth still,
Something more than mortal courage,
  Something more than human will.

Oh that they could learn to conquer!
  Oh that they could come to know
How the truer way is opened
  To the bosom of a foe!

Not by bars of steel and iron,
  Not by rack and torture here,
Can ye force the higher spirit
  From its great and only sphere.

Throw your prison-gates asunder,
  Strike the iron from his hand,
Bid him walk the earth a freeman,
  Make him equal in the land;

Show him first that you are noble,
  Let him see that you are brave,
Act no longer as a coward,
  Be not brutal as a slave.

While he lingers in the shackles
  He is master of you all,
He is freer than the sentry
  In your very prison-hall;
          M *

He is better, prouder, freer
  Than the proudest of your State;
He can teach you what is noble,
  He can show you what is great.

May the angels at his pillow
  Their undying vigils keep!
God preserve his Southern children,
  Who are praying as they weep!

*   *   *   *   *   *

As the fire hid in ashes
  Under mountains of the earth,
When its red volcanic lava
  Struggles into upper birth,

There are words that come unbidden,
  And the lips are burst apart
By a passion leaping upward
  From its covert in the heart.

Though we bury wrongs, to hide them
  From our own and other eyes,
There are those that in us quicken,
  For the spirit never dies;

And upward from the charnel
  Come the living that were dead,
All the olden wounds upon them,
  All the marks of where they bled.

Oh that crimes and wrongs were fewer !
Oh that men were better grown !
Oh that veins had less of fever !
Oh that hearts had less of stone !

*　　*　　*　　*　　*　　*

Brave Kentucky ! brave, but laggard
　　When her sisters gave their blood,
She has walked into the current
　　With her bosom to the flood ;

She has dared to give example
　　To the cruel-hearted States,
When she meets her Southern children
　　With a welcome at her gates.

Though a tyrant held her silent
　　In the shadow of her guns,
She had all a mother's yearning
　　For the glory of her sons ;

And with chains upon her person,
　　And a hand upon her mouth,
She had not a pulse within her
　　But was beating for the South.

Better far than poor Missouri,
　　Better far than Tennessee,
And Virginia, best of any,
　　Better now than she.

Ah, Virginia! torn and bleeding,
　　O'er the ashes of her dead
Let the tears of queenly woman
　　Be the requiem that is said.

Though they build no pallid marble
　　O'er the silence of their graves,
There are tombs in fairer bosoms
　　For Virginia's fallen braves.

Pass, O seasons, spring and summer!
　　Come again, O winter cold!
Time shall never lose the record,
　　Time shall hear the story told!

Truth has more of spirit-feature,
　　Falsehood more of human cast;
Nations yet unborn shall hear it,
　　Truth shall conquer at the last.

LEE.

We saw the fragile maiden, May,
  Trip down the paths of morning,
And queen July in central day,
  Her flower-throne adorning;

And weeping trees in sombre lines
  Took up an anthem murmur,
When August, with her trailing vines,
  Went out the gates of Summer.

Now yellow husks are on the grain,
  And leaves are brown and sober,
And sundown clouds have caught again
  The flush of ripe October;

We hear the woody hill-tops croon,
  The airy maize-blades whisper,
The year is in its afternoon,
  And leaf-bells ring the vesper.

What is it gives this gloaming-song
    Its melancholy feature?
What is it makes our souls prolong
    This monotone of nature?

What tearful grief is in our hearts —
    What swaying under-reason?
What sorrow real now imparts
    Its spirits to the season?

The crisping leaves may shoal the ways,
    The sun turn down the heavens —
Still all the years have fading days,
    And all the days have evens:

Enough — whatever else may be —
    That in this autumn weather,
The verdure of the world and LEE
    Have silent fled together.

So prone are men where'er they move
    To tread the ways of evil,
They seldom hold their kind above
    A common grade and level;

But LEE, beside his fellow-man,
    Stood, over all, a giant —
The higher type — the perfect plan —
    God fearing, God-reliant.

A giant not alone in fields
Where bent· the sanguine Reaper,
Where Death threw o'er his harvest-yields
An autumn crimson deeper;

But with the iron strength of will
He sought his life to fashion;
He held his ruder pulses still,
And closed the gates of passion.

There have been men whose mighty deeds,
On cold historic pages,
Are driven like October seeds
Along the reaching ages;

Whose statues stand like sentinels,
On whitened shafts and bases,
Whose ashes rest in marble cells,
And sepulchres and vases;

But he who in this autumn time
Was lost beyond the river,
Has found a glory-path to climb,
Forever and forever!

And monumental marble here,
With deeds of honor graven,
What can it be to one so near
The inner gates of Heaven?

By still Potomac's margin dun,
　Where shrilly calls the plover,
Where lean the heights of Arlington
　Its glassing waters over,

No autumn voices haunt the moles,
　No breezy covert ripples,
No longer whirl the leaves in shoals
　Beneath the stately maples;

Some vandal's axe has shorn the crest,
　The woody slopes are shaven,
No longer builds the dove her nest
　Where mournful croaks the raven;

But down the Southland's fruity plain
　The leaves are all a-quiver,
And *there* his memory shall reign
　Forever and forever!

NOTES.

I⊤ was not thought necessary to introduce these poems with any apologetic preface, as no apology ought to excuse an act of this kind ; but the author takes advantage of these notes to say that his verses are an accumulation of the rubbish of boyhood and youth, mixed with a few expressions of his later manhood. A demand for such a collection has existed among his friends for several years, and he has taken advantage of terms offered by his publisher to prepare this volume, without a further design than that of gratifying those who have manifested a personal interest in him and his writings.

The poem entitled LEE, was hastily prepared after this book was ready for press. The subject was worthy a far higher tribute than any tongue or pen could offer ; but those who know the author will see in the lines a *desire* to do honor to the memory of the great and good man ; and what more can be done ?

SHE appeared in the *Yeoman*, at Frankfort, Ky., in August last. It was severely handled by a writer in the *Cincinnati Enquirer*, who thought "for the sake of letters," poetry of that sentiment had better not be encouraged. It was evident from the character of the paragraphs, that he who wrote was perhaps as appreciative of the lines as the author himself. The poem, if it may be called such, was never intended for any other purpose than that of eliciting remark. It succeeded in this particular case, if not in general.

The poems SIXTY-FIVE and SIXTY-SIX, were written in the years indicated, and published as New Year addresses. The apostrophe to Kentucky in the last poem, was occasioned by the circumstance of the repeal of an Expatriation law by the Legislature.

The MONEYLESS MAN appeared for the first time in 1855.

The BIVOUAC pictures a condition of the Confederate soldiery as existing at Bull's Gap, in 1862.

UNDER THE PINES was produced on an outpost near the City of Richmond, one night in 1864.

The lines entitled HIS LAST DAY, were written upon a few hours' notice, and read at the closing exercises of Rosemont Academy. Mr. W. W. Richeson, the tutor, had been in charge of a school at Maysville, Ky., for thirty-seven years, and this occasion was the last upon which he would officiate there in that capacity. He had taught the parents and grand-parents of some of his scholars, and was greatly beloved in the community.

The lines addressed to MASTER GEO. W. JOHNSTON, were written on his birthday. He was then twelve years of age, and had already distinguished himself by a long retention of a place on the "roll of honor" at an excellent school. His development of character now gives high promise of later worth.

FALLEN was one of the author's early efforts. It was first published in the *Illustrated News* at Richmond, Va., in 1862, but had been written several years before.

THE LITTLE BOY GUIDING THE PLOW was written at "Tally's Church," a small log-house in East Tennessee, in 1864. The condition of that section at the time was such as the poem represents.

A lady of Virginia gave the author a NASTURTIUM FLOWER in memory of Swain's conceit —

"A spirit dwells in every flower."

She said a fairy inhabited the one she gave, which she hoped would inspire a poem. The verses were written in camp that night.

THE FAITH SHE PLIGHTED ME is founded upon an actual circumstance. The unfortunate gentleman, however, still lives, having fairly forgotten his disappointment in the possession of a new love.